1.2

Raintree Rhymers

Book One

Humpty Dumpty
Jack and Jill
Three Blind Mice

Raintree Childrens Books

Text copyright © 1986 Raintree Publishers Inc.

Illustrations copyright © 1981 Ginn and Company Ltd.

Library of Congress Number: 85-12429

Library of Congress Cataloging in Publication Data
Main entry under title:
  Raintree rhymers.

  Summary: Four books include familiar nursery rhymes
such as "Humpty Dumpty," "Little Miss Muffet," and
"Rain, Rain, Go Away," accompanied by activity pages
with rhyming exercises for beginning readers.
  1. Nursery rhymes.   2. Children's poetry.
[1. Nursery rhymes]
PZ8.3.R145   1985   398'.8   85-12429

ISBN 0-8172-2451-3 (lib. bdg.)
ISBN 0-8172-2456-4 (softcover)

2 3 4 5 6 7 8 9 10   90 89 88 87 86

Humpty Dumpty

Humpty Dumpty sat on a wall.

Humpty Dumpty had a great fall.

All the king's horses

And all the king's men

Couldn't put Humpty together again.

9

Humpty Dumpty sat on a wall.

Humpty Dumpty had a great fall.

All the king's horses

And all the king's men

Couldn't put Humpty together again.

It Sounds Like . . .

Words that rhyme sound alike, like *ball, fall, wall.*
Think of words that sound like **men, wall,** and **boat.**
These three poems will help you.

1. To think of a word
   That sounds like **men,**
   Think of soft yellow chicks
   And the mother _____ .

2. To think of a word
   That sounds like **wall,**
   Think of how short you are
   And how your dad is _____ .

3. To think of a word
   That sounds like **boat,**
   Think of going to a farm
   And seeing a _____ .

Write a Poem

Now, finish these three poems. Choose a word for each blank. Your word should sound like the word in capital letters.

1. An egg is easy to break, you KNOW.
   It's made of shell from head to _____ .

2. If you ever see an egg on a WALL,
   Tell him to be sure he doesn't _____ .

3. There's an egg on the wall. What a SIGHT!
   He's been sitting there all day and all _____ .

Jack and Jill

Jack and Jill went up the hill

To fetch a pail of water.

Jack fell down

And broke his crown,

And Jill came tumbling after.

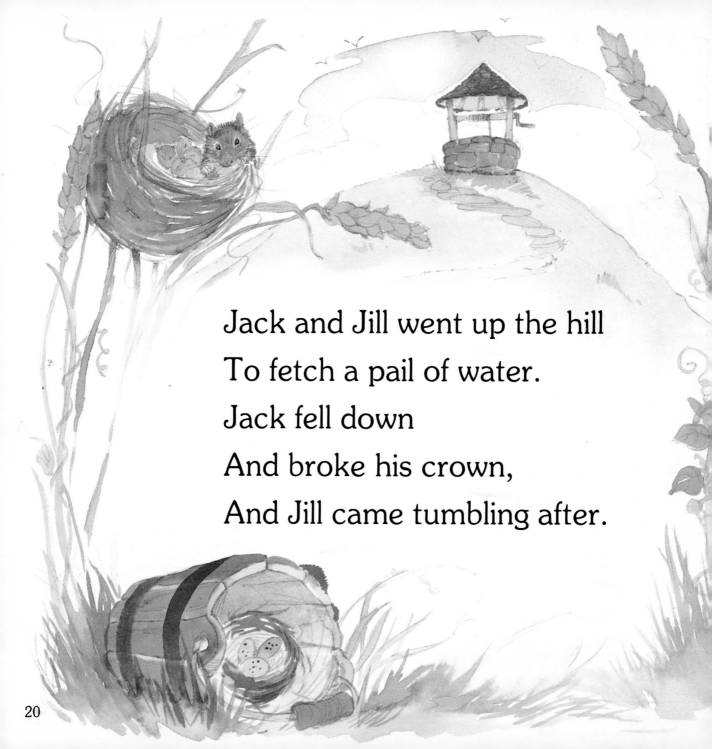

Jack and Jill went up the hill
To fetch a pail of water.
Jack fell down
And broke his crown,
And Jill came tumbling after.

It Sounds Like . . .

Words that rhyme, sound alike, like *hill, Bill, Jill.*
Think of words that sound like **came, broke,** and **pail.**
These three poems will help you.

1. To think of a word
   That sounds like **came,**
   Think of when you write
   Your very own _____ .

2. To think of a word
   That sounds like **broke,**
   Think of when you tell
   A funny _____ .

3. To think of a word
   That sounds like **pail,**
   Think of a little brown dog
   That is wagging its _____ .

Write a Poem

Now, finish these three poems. Choose a word for each blank. Your word should sound like the word in capital letters.

1. The sky is blue. Jack's pants are, TOO.
The patches show they are not _____ .

2. Jack and Jill went to the WELL
To fill their pail and ring the _____ .

3. Jack fell down and hurt his HEAD.
He went off crying and home to _____ .

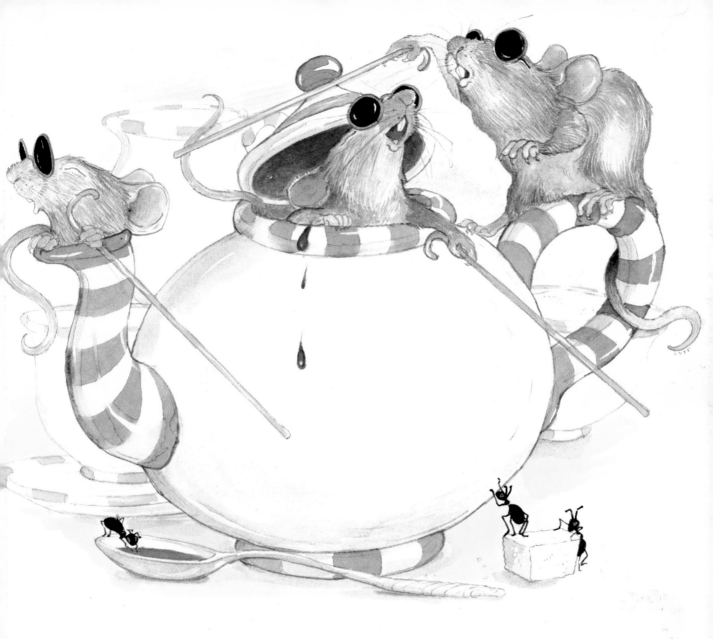

Three Blind Mice

Three blind mice,
Three blind mice,

24

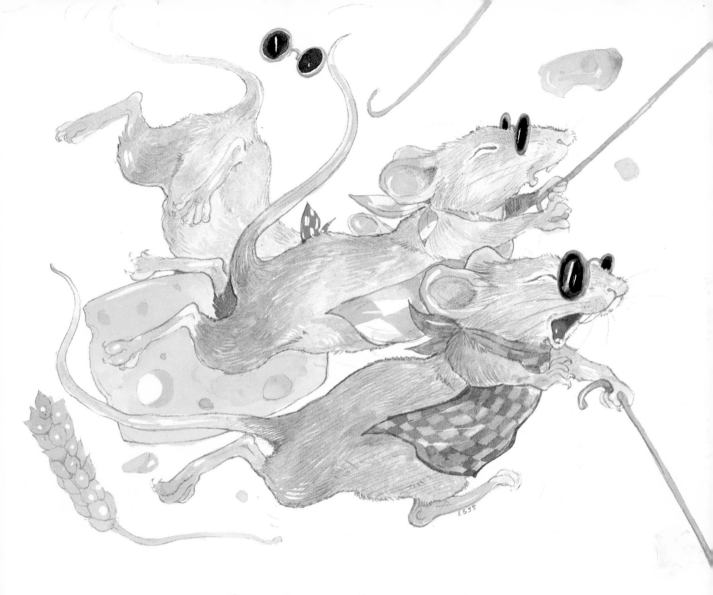

See how they run!
See how they run!

They all ran after
The farmer's wife,

Who cut off their tails
With a carving knife.

Did you ever see
Such a sight in your life

As three blind mice?

Three blind mice,
Three blind mice,
See how they run!
See how they run!
They all ran after
The farmer's wife,
Who cut off their tails
With a carving knife.
Did you ever see
Such a sight in your life
As three blind mice?

It Sounds Like . . .

Words that rhyme, sound alike, like *mice, rice, nice.*
Think of words that sound like **mice, tail,** and **blind.**
These three poems will help you.

1. To think of a word
   That sounds like **mice,**
   Think of a snowman,
   Who is cold as _____ .

2. To think of a word
   That sounds like **tail,**
   Think of using
   A hammer and _____ .

3. To think of a word
   That sounds like **blind,**
   Think of someone who is
   Friendly and _____ .

Write a Poem

Now, finish these three poems. Choose a word for each blank. Your word should sound like the word in capital letters.

1. If you know a mouse that you want to PLEASE,
   Just give him a great big piece of _____ .

2. A mouse has a tail that is long and THIN.
   In fact, it's so long, it can touch his _____ .

3. It's a very unusual thing, that's PLAIN . . .
   A mouse wearing glasses and carrying a _____ .